GOOD MORNING, CITY

BY ELAINE MOORE · PICTURES BY WILLIAM LOW

Troll

BridgeWater Paperback

First paperback edition published in 2002.

Text copyright © 1995 by Elaine Moore.

Illustrations copyright © 1995 by William Low.

Published by BridgeWater Paperback, an imprint
of Troll Communications, L.L.C.

Published in hardcover by BridgeWater Books.

Printed in the United States of America.

10 9 8 7 6 5 4 3 2

**Library of Congress
Catologing-in-Publication Data**

Moore, Elaine.
Good morning, city / by Elaine Moore;
pictures by William Low.
p.   cm.
Summary: Depicts morning in the city as
people go to work and children go to school.
ISBN 0-8167-3654-5 (lib.bdg.) ISBN 0-8167-3655-3 (pbk.)
[1. City and town life—Fiction.   2. Morning—
Fiction.]   1. Low, William, ill.   II. Title.
PZ7.M7832Gk 1995 [Fic]—dc20 94-35458

For Cheryll Chew, John Frye,
and Kalli Dakos
E.M.

For my friend, Yiorgos
W.L.

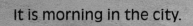

It is morning in the city.

In the middle of the city, the sky is silver gray
like the inside of a pot.
The sun cannot be seen.
That's because the buildings are high
and block out the sun.
But it is still morning in the city.

In the hospital, doctors can't see the sun either.
They look at the clock to know it is morning.
They yawn because they are tired from working all night long.
They worked the night shift.
Soon other doctors will work the day shift
while the weary night shift sleeps.

At the edge of the city, fog lifts slowly off the river
as the shadow of a tall ship creeps toward the bridge.
The bridge attendant raises the bridge
while a foghorn makes its muffled sound.
Welcome to our city, tall ship.

The sun is rising in the sky as truck drivers
slam shut the heavy doors on their eighteen-wheelers.
They clang the iron bars down, fastening them
so the metal doors won't fly open when they ride the highway home.
Inside the supermarket, stock boys line shelves with groceries.
It is morning, but it is early—too early to open the grocery.

It is not too early to open a donut shop.
It is not too soon to bake donuts or place them,
smelling sugary and delicious, on wire racks behind the counter.
Hot from working in the kitchen, the baker pauses
to watch customers eating his fresh, warm donuts.
Happily, the baker fills the wire racks again and again and again.
Two chocolate donuts, please!

Near the park, street cleaners shut down their machines.
With a creak and a groan they raise the stiff bristle brushes
that last night scrubbed the streets and gutters clean.
Leaving, they wave to sanitation workers
who drive loud, clanking dumpsters.
Now as the sun continues to climb, it is their turn
to clean the city's streets.

Down below, under the street, subway attendants cannot know
that the sky is turning as blue as a teacup.
From the underground world of the subway,
they cannot see or hear the upstairs world of the city.
Only the rumble and whir and hissing steam of the subway train.
Only the echoes of voices
as people pass through the yellow haze to catch their trains.
In the subway, workers listen to radios
to learn what is happening in the city.

It is not all hustle and bustle.
In the city, there is a tall stone building
with steep points called steeples
and cathedral bells that harken each new day.
There it is peaceful and calm.
Now as bells peal, people stand on the stone steps
and blink in the light of the risen sun.

High above, construction crews
climb girders and platforms.
Some ride cranes that swing beams of steel.
Workers wait, their faces streaked with sweat,
when it is still morning and the day has just begun.
They try not to look down.
From where they stand, the people below
look like bugs darting across a pond.
Big trucks are sandbox toys.

In the middle of the city, sunlight floods
the corner of First and Main.
Horns honk. Tires squeal.
People hurry to work
in the tall buildings and small shops
that line the busy streets.
A police officer whistles.
Teams of people rush across the street.

A traffic light blinks red
and a yellow school bus stops.
Its rubber lips open and whoosh shut
after the children climb on.
From inside the bus, they listen
as the police officer whistles again.
Rumble, rumble. The bus rumbles on its way.

People go to work.
Children go to school.
It is morning in the city.

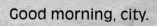

Good morning, city.